A Sky Full

of

Blobby Mountains

by
John Hulme

First paperback edition

ISBNs:
Paperback: 978-1-80227-766-1
ebook: 978-1-80227-767-8

To Sharin,
Hoping there's a hidden gem
or two here for you.
John

A Sky Full
of
Blobby Mountains

John Hulme
May 2024

Contents

A new kind of sad

What if you sobbed out a new kind of sad?

A funny kind of,
puffy kind of,
frowny kind of face,
deep in those caverns, deep in your heart,
where
all of the voices insist that you smile...
because
hopelessness here is the end of the line.

What if you had the kind of sad
that burrowed you down
to a bottomless place?

What if you had a kind of sad
that turns the little spindle
on the pavement where you stand?

What if your sad was like a trapeze?

Lifting you,
spinning you,
flipping you round

out through a street full of dead brick and glass
and all of those things
that you know you can't be.

What if you had the kind of sad
that saw where it hurts
and held where it stings
and twirled you
and turned you
and dropped your soul free?

What if your sad was a river?

What if the planet would shake when you sobbed,

feeling the weight of unspeakable things?

What if your sad made you shimmer and shine?

Refashioned your hands into rivers and pens

and scribbled their stories all over the fens?

What if you had the kind of sad
that made the world
softer
and wove you back home?

Even though you somehow know
your heart has nowhere left to go...

What if your tears were actually made

of tassels
and castles
and towers twisted out of dew

and all those sacred things that grow

out in the sad place
that won't let you go...

speckled with scarlet
and
carpets of green
and bright pools of yellow
where giants have been...

out in those heartbreaking mountain ravines
for
all of the deepest unsayable things
where
fur-coated tree creatures
scuttle and play...

where tentacle branches
and
root-jointed claws
will
dance with those screaming things
deep in your eyes

and paint all those galaxies,
lifetimes away,
with something you just have to tell them today.

What if you sobbed out a new kind of sad,

What if you held it and made it your own?

What if your raindrops
and all of your tears...
and of your cloud-hugging blobby-rock mountains,
all of your forests
and all of your streams...

what if
all of these spells
that you paint out your tears on

were allergic to all of those everyday shelves?

Those everyday shelves made of everyday life

that get shoved in the way when the rain's coming down.

Splash night

I remember the night as though it swept in only yesterday - as though its fingers were still digging, ever so gently, into my shoulder.

I saw the thing I loved most in myself, climbing out of me like a joyful fountain and skipping lightly over the shoreside rocks.

I saw the thing I craved, waiting for me beneath a full moon, dripping with wet glow and shaking herself against the backlit blue. She was like a nightlight, a bedtime story...

a taste of home in a galaxy that would always be staying out too late.

She hung there on glistening ropes of moonbeam, smiling mischievously into my insatiable eyes as though I was watching her in defiance of some cosmic law. But there was nothing smug or knowing about that smile. It was a fragile thing, like all the treasures that had ever caught me unawares.

I gazed at her with my jittery, spellbound eyes. I watched her peeking into all my private adventures through her secret spyhole in the sky; a thing so soft, so essential, that I knew I couldn't last the night without holding her; a thing that could carry me from here to forever if I asked her right.

Moonbeams flared and twirled in her smoky luminescence, highlighting the spot where she hovered over the beach, and as she danced there, her arms made wave after wave of ripple patterns in the surrounding blueness.

Her light was subtle and real and fresh –

raw in a good way, with a wholeness that made me want to run, to skip weightlessly over everything solid and stone-like, just the way she was doing.

I sprinted, leapt up, tried to catch her ripples out of the air. I wanted them with a kind of bottomless passion, perhaps like something an overfed star might feel when the whole Universe was exhorting it to burn. Yet there was a gentleness about it, too - the kind of desire that makes you feel pure again, even when it tickles you in the deepest and naughtiest of forbidden places.

Somehow, I had always known she was there, dancing me away from myself, laughing at the way my chipped and crumbling soul continued to rebuild itself against every new tide. She was like a secret heartbeat, a rhythm nestled in a rhythm, purring contentedly behind the things I never said.

But suddenly, I needed her touch more than I had ever done. I needed her to be real and ragged and achingly visceral, just like I was. I needed those thighs of hers not simply to perch on that ethereal window ledge but to exist, in all their soft, authentic majesty, sweaty and firm and uncompromising against the bottomless night beyond.

I needed to know, when I wore her in the days to come, that she at least might be the one real friend to whom I could always come home. There would always, I knew, be meaner visions to undermine her. Darker tides would one day be coming from all those unlit faraway places. But it was the shadowy presences close to home that scared me the most.

I needed her because she had a touch of the same darkness, like sad sparks catching in her eyes...

and in my chest.

Her smile never wavered, though, as she twirled and twisted on those moonbeam ropes: half starlight, half bonfire, unzipping her private place in the sky so that plumes of undefined mischief might grin their way free and float off into the night.

I wanted to drink her ethereal skin so I could breathe again. I wanted to lose myself in the folds of nightlit air and rediscover hope. I wanted her to honour the best in me for my devotion, and I yearned for the scolding touch of her lightning fingers as penance for every other wasted night.

"So, go on, then," I taunted, hearing the tide start to roll in, feeling it saturate the sand behind my shoes. "Push me!"

I didn't want to pace the waterline. Not that night. Not with my true love watching. Just this once, I didn't want to settle for a halfway place, aching and screaming between one world and another...

a halfway place where nothing is ever truly claimed.

"Push me! Push me in!" I yelled again.

I felf a shove, gentle as a wisp of cloud, hard as a sea-mist fist, and I dropped like a stone, into a cauldron of surf and sand.

Currents and lights swirled and bubbled around me - jellyfish headlights and plankton auroras and bins full of burning seaweed for itinerant tide-burrowers to pause and warm their hands on.

I felt the warmth of distant suns.

I felt the coolness of monsoon rains over vast forests.

I felt the breathlessness of rivers, cutting their stories through the mountains.

But most of all, I felt the thing I loved, the thing I held inside myself and outside my tender skies, phosphorescing in the bubbles I was half sitting, half floating in, pulling a part of my soul clear out of itself.

I felt...

shellshocked.

I lay there, swishing and swirling, for an endless, excruciating minute, wondering why I was always compelled to snatch up such treasures, only to drag them down into the messiest, dirtiest of places. The minute stretched me all the way to forever and back, before slowly hauling me back to my feet.

Wetness dripped heavily from my clothes, chortling and giggling at my inability to keep a beautiful thing from soiling itself in my hands, howling at the brazen impudence of my craziness.

Somehow, though, I refused to be humiliated. Even in a world as harsh as this one, some treasures are worth their messier selves.

As I dragged myself soaked and dripping from the beach, scuttling home to lock my secret love away, page after page of grinning heartache was unzipping itself from the sodden sea cloud I had become. Page after page, poem after poem, story after story... I rained myself over the footpath, up from the shore. I rained myself over the pavement, my squelchy shoes treading that heavy line between delight and embarrassment.

I rained myself in through the back door, splashed myself into the bathroom and curled up in the tub,

smiling in a way I would never smile again.

Hop song

Not many people knew about my romance with Fawn. We kept it wrapped up all snug and secret in a tight little pendant which neither of us took off, and which only we could open, guarded as it was by one of those secret floral combinations that the old forest scribes once used to write the corners of galaxies into flower petals.

Not that most people would have been interested enough to break the code.

You'd think, given the nature of our relationship, that we'd have been the talk of the town back then, given the way we used to hop everywhere like a couple of demented cartoon bunnies.

Surprisingly, though, most people seemed unable or unwilling to see us, hopping down the street, hopping through the supermarket aisles, hopping into all the little offices where various mean-spirited little regulations were increasingly being implemented in an attempt to frame our lives in more static terms.

We hopped through phone calls from people who had better ideas about what we should be doing with our lives.

We hopped through conversations with people whose movement was so much more purposeful and so much less random.

We hopped through conversations where people explained what was wrong with the world and why society would start to function so much better if people learned when not to crash into things and when to sit still in chairs.

We listened to people who saw life through much better lenses, and people who could twist the hopping speckles in our eyes into sensible patterns, so that we might see the world we were supposed to see, and live the way we were supposed to live.

We listened to people who scrutinised the lack of narrative in our files, who challenged our insistence on wobbling off message and bouncing against the margins, without ever questioning why the world had exiled us there in the first place.

We hopped down filthy alleys, looking for things we'd been forced to throw away and would probably never find again.

We hopped in strange, intimate circles 'til our feet bled, often enticing sad, shabby people out of the shadows as we did so.

They wept and smiled every time they saw us.

Sometimes they showered us with reckless kisses until we stumbled in the overwhelming presence of their need - only to haul us back to our feet and scream at us to dance more...

and more...

and more...

They pushed us through streets and gates and nervous doors in the hope that our hop dance might leave a kinder rhythm on the world's stale air.

And we would cry from exhaustion.

And another part of the pendant would crack.

Most of the time, we would never see such people again. Or if we did, there would be only the tiniest specks of recognition in what was left of their faces, damp behind eyes in which all the lights had been turned off.

We retreated to the woods, hopping over soft mossy carpets and spongy bark trampolines and bouncing up the side of massive trees, switching on lichen-powered fairy lights as we did so.

But the trees grew stale and the lights went out. Their passing would haunt us as branches broke beneath our ill-equipped feet.

We hopped along beaches, tapping out a shell-crunch drumbeat against the bolder melodies of the tide. We scattered phosphorescent fireworks as the spray danced off our bouncing bodies.

We hopped over each other's skin, stretching as we did so, opening up places that had lingered unspoken and undiscovered in our consciousness for far too long. We punctuated each other's aches and passions with our secret spring-footed choreography, and the world's tiniest secrets began to tremble at the pulsating warmth of our embrace.

We bounced into places where no stillness could ever settle, and we bled a little in places that people still don't talk about at dinner parties.

We bled so wild and so deep that the Universe still talks about us over coffee and burnt-out stars.

Right now, however, I just walk a lot, generally through places I don't want to be, waiting for the moment when I can't take any more. There is a screaming inside me, so much louder than it was before, and a dizziness that refuses to go away.

I carry a little weeping backpack in the quietest corner of my imagination, and some days even that becomes too heavy a burden to ignore.

Every so often, I try to put it back on, to hop with it the way I used to, back when the desperation for trampoline truth was all I had... but the tears and the memories are just too heavy, and the springs are all broken.

The phrase "I wish I could help you" echoes everywhere, though it rarely lands with any kind of sincerity. I have seen too much of what this world thinks help looks like.

What they really wish is that the hopping would stop. I know that.

Even now, they can still see the galaxies wobbling behind my eyes.

I have Fawn's heartbeat locked in a pendant. I have the snores of vast, sleeping dragons in my feet. I have words that bounce along the ripples of lakes like stones skimming across a page.

You go to lakes whose tried-and-tested ripples you can see and feel, and you sit there in your little boats, wondering why I chose not to come with you... wondering why I always stand on the shoreline, why I never buy tickets to real places.

You have so many better answers to all the questions I wasn't trying to ask. But there are real places... and there are genuine places -

and there's an awful long wait on the shoreline between the two.

Every so often, a familiar texture catches me by surprise, teasing some of the old hoppy rhythm to the surface. A tiny mechanism shifts and sobs on a necklace chain, and rusted gears click back into sync, just enough to unlock a piece of the pendant and claw a few echoes of the dance back.

Every so often, I still feel the hopping places. Every so often, I'm not curled up in a shrieking ball of words that only a handful of readers have the stomach for.

But sometimes, in the middle of all the probes and prods of a bounceless yet relentless little world, spoiled by the illusion of its bigness, even my own words become too painful to hold without hating them just a little.

Lanterns and songs

Sometimes, I think my heart is made of songs -

much like this one I'm dancing to right now.

Sometimes, I think the night air is a tapestry, woven out of undiscovered music, just wild enough to dance away the days that break my heart.

Sometimes, I think every single thread of night air is stitched out of one street corner, several million blocks away, where the rest of the world left me behind and everything became clear…

where my feet became lanterns in the echoes of conversations I could never have again.

Dancing away the echoes is easy.

Most of those nights weren't half as beautiful as they felt when I was leaving them. Some of them were downright toxic, as such nights all-too-often are. Laughter is an easy thing to dissolve, once you know the joke was never really that funny to begin with.

But dancing away the ghosts -

the ghosts I carry around like lanterns, because of a light that stained the night so deeply it'll never wash off -

that's much harder.

I'm a notebook now, with candles woven into the pages... and I'm still struggling to find my way home. I'm a journal, writing itself down unfamiliar streets, and sometimes I think every single page is haunted -

which is perhaps why a part of me is always dancing in the margins...

and why all the best songs are written between the lines...

like a squirrel swinging and crashing between branches,

singing the songs there are no words for.

On the bad days

It's when I can't make a phone call
that everyone else assumes should be easy.
It's when I'm too nervous to drive down a road
that nobody else sees a problem with,
or too nervous to say hello to someone
who everyone else tells me
thinks the world of me.
It's when I need to cry like a broken tap
and just not stop,
but the churn stops halfway up my throat
and won't let go.
It's when the world just beyond the window
looks way too beautiful to ignore
but way too scary to step in.
It's when one little compliment
feels like a Nobel Peace Prize
wrapped up in all my birthdays,
all come at once.
It's when filling in that form
is like trying to write my name in a language I don't know
with a barbed wire pen.

On a bad day, it's like that.

And it screams and it stabs
and it scratches me raw.

Even while I catch snowflakes made of starlight and dewdrop
and write small stories
in a ripple I smuggled home from the tide.

Even when it's as beautiful as this...

and as nasty as that.

On a bad day,
bits of me dance
just like they do on a good day,

except for a gazillion holes in my spacesuit

and a bottomless ache in my heart,
watching me decompress in explosive slow motion.

And it's so hard to explain
without losing too much of myself in translation
or sounding like I'm saying something I'm really not.

And it's none of those things they tell me it is.

So I sit here,
grateful for those moments when it breaks

and I can cry again...

all the way down the wall to freedom.

And I know that the world would be so much less

without these nasty little miracles I spend the bad days riding out.

Shoe-song night

An ache...

a hope...

Not an egret
or a heron,
gorgeous as they are.

Not a swoop,
wide open wings.

It's not your dog again
tonight,
awesome as those cuddles are,

gentle as the tongue,
the nuzzle,
the sniff...

the furry explosions of "hello!"

Not a sunset,
a paintbox
woven out of fire.

Not the river,
galloping down that mountain trail.

Not the tide,
the gallop of oceans,
cantering home.

Just me...

an ache...

and let's stop pretending about the hope.

Just me,

taking it all personally -

all the stuff
they say is not personal.

It's just the system,

just how it is,
just the cogs,
the gears...

It's just the world...

with all the bits I ache for,
filtered
neatly
out.

It's all just standard.

It's not personal.

It's simply...

me,

taking it personal anyway...

taking it all,

so very, very personally.

Because
who else,
what else is there?

It's just who I am.

It's just what I do.

The politics of standing in a shoe
that
doesn't
fit

and dying in stories that lie about it.

Tree stars and love letters

It's night. I'm leaning out of the balcony window, stretching the kitchen into new realms, listening to the river below me, rich and crisp and somehow wilder than all the other adventures the world insists on rubbing in my face...

all the other things I'm told I ought to be doing to validate a joy that always seems to show up on someone else's terms.

None of those things matter now.

Freedom catches me here, after all those games of hide-and-seek we've played.

Freedom catches me here in this place of watching and being, hanging on the edge of a bridge to somewhere else, watching branches that reach towards me like fluffy stars, speckled as they are with shiny blossom.

It's like the night is straining to hug me from the other side of the river...

and it feels so much more me than it did a moment ago.

This is me made whole in a way that the world rarely seems able to accommodate. This is me finally ready for an adventure, now that the rest of the day has played itself out. The stillness is restless and there is a sting in the silence - the stirring of things I almost dare not share, lest someone pulls apart the stitching.

Such things have become my safe place now... my slice of perfect, written in textures just ragged enough to make the spell real.

Two minutes here, and I feel like I have clawed back every piece of precious that was ever stolen from me.

Perhaps these midnight finger blossoms are enough. Perhaps the other hug I am waiting for, the elusive one, will not matter.

But it does. It always does.

Suddenly, like a perfume kicking in from a place I haven't breathed in yet, like a dark flower wearing heavy boots, the dream of you holding me is now the only thing that matters...

whoever you are,

with your face made of tree stars, waiting to surprise me.

Train wheels

For the first month, he sat on trains, rolling from one place to another with the world staring back at him over railway embankments.

He saw distant forests through a milky window,

the green fuzz on hillsides made too lush by the sweep of rain clouds,

distant dark towers, peppered with the nightlights of people whose keys still fit the doors they were designed for,

whose locks never stopped clicking in the right places, and laughing at the right jokes.

He saw the world roll past on tracks,

ladling his old hopes into trundling goods wagons

and wailing mournfully in a language only the freight trains would ever want to understand.

For the second month, he roamed the promenades and the beaches, watching the tide roll in,

hearing the altogether softer clockwork of the open ocean whittle through his heart like a piece of sacrificial driftwood, shedding his ghosts in the shavings

and rekindling old fires in the blade.

He felt his body crunch and bleed on the shingle,

wishing the fury of angry, splintered fists and rootless, restless, scratching fingers could pick the lock on those rotten doors

and set his credentials free.

He cried, gently and prettily, at the silence of shooting stars.

He spent the third month in the company of trees,

bathing his spirit in the benevolence of mossy odours and the crumbling majesty of finely-sculpted bark.

He breathed them in as gently as he could, listening to the stories on each branch, and planted them on the fertile slopes of his lungs -

row after row, like they were family.

Then he coughed and scratched out the memory with those fierce fingers, once he had remembered what that word really meant to him.

Rain-soaked foliage wept, gently and prettily, at the silence of wounded souls.

In the fourth month, they broke down his door,

more to collect overdue heartbeats than anything else.

They found him floating in the silence

between tears and shooting stars and wounded souls.

They found him welded to a chair.

But they never got that lock open,

and they never found any of the stories he used to tell, or the poems he used to write around the edge of train wheels.

Street art

She's still talking, still weaving the story about where she needs to go and how her friend can't take her there on an empty tank...

and how she can't afford the bus ride...

and how she's not been able to eat, and she's not sure where she will be able to sleep because...

and how it's just all gone wrong today...

and she knows it sounds crazy bad luck but... but...

I didn't mean to tune out, given the effort she's putting into the performance.

But all I can see are the dragonflies, tweeting their metallic rainbow beacon-speak at each other as they swoop through the pauses in her speech.

All I can see is the blue-green cloak, mossy velvet pouring over her shoulders in a rainstorm of old stories. Dead stories, maybe. Delusions and fantasies to keep the soul warm...

but the queen still lives there anyway, in her eyes. The queen still wears her cloak, and she still sees me as I used to be, just a heartbeat ago, before the last piece of hope began to burn.

I have nothing but embers now, and she has dragonflies.

I didn't mean to tune out, garbage though I know her story is. But the weight of tears between us is too great, because I know she sees it in me, even if I can no longer see it in myself. I know she sees where our colours and our dragonflies meet, and I feel the spark there.

I know she aches for the same bridge as I do, and I know she sees me seeing her, just as she'll always be -

once you push past the shabby curtains these streets have drawn around her eyes.

Heck, she hasn't taken her eyes off me once.

I reach into my pocket, figure out what I need to get me through the rest of the day, and find myself halving it, for no reason I could even begin to explain to all those cynical survivalist voices in my head. I take out a couple of notes and press them into her wavering fingers.

She hasn't even got to the punchline yet, but I know what she's angling for, and she knows I know.

She wells up, launching into a pirouette of thank yous, and plants several kisses on my cheek.

It's a busy street, and a couple of the shoppers are watching the embrace with barely-concealed distaste.

Their eyes take in the matted hair, the scabs and the poorly-nourished look, and their value system processes its significance.

They give me the "I suppose you know what she's going to spend that on" look, and they're clearly wondering how I can return the hug without feeling sick.

A small flock of dragonflies dissolve in their value judgenents.

I know the story she gave me wasn't true. She knows I know.

But if my own stumbles have taught me anything, it's that the truth of a moment is rarely anything to do with the truth of a moment.

Go figure.

The whole tableau leaves me feeling dirty as I walk away - though not for the reasons that all the columnists and influencers will be writing about when tomorrow's opinions are wheeled out for public consumption - and I push my own tears back down into their hiding place.

At least for now, I tell myself. Something inside is telling me I still have better places to put them.

If only it were always that simple.

But today, it kind of is.

Raining back up

Sometimes, I need that bouncing smile more than anything.

You know the one - the smile that bounces back at you when you see someone and they see you back.

Sometimes, I need it so much... so deeply.

Sometimes it'll lift me, fill in the holes where I've been crumbling. Sometimes it'll be the thing that makes me cry.

They say that soft, gentle rain is the worst kind of rain for soaking you past the point of no return...

but there's a softer, kinder, deeper kind of rain than that.

There's the rain that lives inside our eyes, lighting beacons in those moments when being seen is worth everything...

and being the warrior who's too cool to acknowledge your attention means nothing.

I have a friend who cries when a bird flies unexpectedly into her camera lens, who cries when she finds herself capturing a moment she wasn't meant to hold on to.

She cried when she took the pelican flying over the boat she was on, and she sent it to me, knowing how much I would love it.

She sent it as a tribute to a pelican I keep with me, like an angel in a locket. I saw it from a whalewatch boat on the Pacific, and wove it through the opening lines of a poem.

I read it at my mum's funeral, when I was too numb and conflicted to cry.

But lately, I've cried a lot over pelicans and angels and herons and the small lockets where I keep incredible things...

folded, precious things.

I read today that folding a thousand cranes will grant you a wish. The cranes that live in my imagination are the wrong kind, I think - not the feathered kind, but the creaky rusted kind, looming like dinosaurs over old dockyards...

waiting for distant ships to see their beacons in places where nobody lights lanterns anymore.

It probably makes me a sucky warrior, dissolving into so much softness, while the world continually hammers the illusion of resilience into our hearts. But surely the world has more than enough warriors right now.

I think real revolution is telling the stories nobody expects to hear...

letting their rain pour out and puddle in the refreshingly pageless space beyond the margins...

and finding yourself seen on the far end of them.

Because your opinion matters

Stand a little,
watching the mountains roll away
and
thinking of all those places
that tripped so easily off your tongue.

Maybe write a treatment -
revised for the screen,
the way all adventures are these days.

Because your opinion matters.

Take a shell home
and keep the pattern under your pillow,
long after the shell has cracked.
Throw a pebble,
watch it drop.

Lose your regrets where the ripples go.

It's a far more honest blue
than any of those one-liner lifelines they've been throwing you.

Because your opinion matters.

Laugh when you feel the beauty.
Cry when you feel the ache.
Be the things

that catch you
when they ripen on your tears -

like a tiny shoot of soft new growth,
wobbling on the breeze,
holding the truth
of all that you've been

and blooming into words that will always,
always
come out wrong.

Because your opinion matters.

Hold that shore you reached for -
the one you only ever saw in silhouette
(and earphones
that now feel mean against your head).
Shake it like a snowglobe
and
go there anyway.

Even when the gesture feels empty,
go there
for all the floating,
swirling snow
that never got away.

Because your opinion matters.

A tree leans close
to hold you,
sharing a root that will never be yours...
blessing your soul
through the next hundred doors...

shrouding your stillness in blossom.

The branch lights up like lightning
so the sun can kiss you one last time.

Because your opinion matters.

It says so right here at the top of the form.

Hope

Whatever my dream was, the alarm killed it.

I woke up.
I hit the alarm.
I checked the window.
Still a little shadowy outside.

Still a little cold.

The smell of hope died a little on my bedclothes.

But I got up anyway, woke myself against the chill of lukewarm water at the sink, made myself a brew and looked, somewhat half-heartedly, for the letter.

I had an appointment in a couple of hours. The letter had kicked off by telling me, somewhat snottily, that they had tried and failed several times to get hold of me by phone, which was weird for a start. I wasn't above turning my phone off or dodging messages when pushed, but there were no missed messages logged on my phone.

Probably a standard letter, I told myself. They probably do this to everyone - phone-scare you into submission.

The letter listed a bunch of documents I was expected to bring with me to the meeting. I didn't recognise the address, but I looked it up in my creased and out-of-date road map.

I didn't have high hopes for the meeting, but my caseworker had told me it was a mere formality, so how bad could it be? So I held on to that tiny crumb of hope during breakfast, ignoring the vague sting in my eyes, grabbed some reasonably freshly-laundered clothes, brushed my teeth in the bathroom mirror and stepped out into the street.

As always, I could feel my little life closing behind me as I shut the front door. I knew this would probably be the biggest I felt all day.

It didn't take me long to find the place, even in what was left of my car (which, despite the look of it, still had a decent enough engine - good enough to tick "own car" for a while when applying for jobs).

For all my misgivings, I was keeping a careful eye on the time. I didn't know which of the stories I had heard about the penalties inflicted for showing up late were actually true, but I really didn't need any more things to stress over. So, never having been to this building before, I had been careful to get there as early as possible so I would be sure to find somewhere to park - never easy this close to the town centre.

The next trick was finding the right entrance.

It was hardly the most prepossessing street, and there was little evidence of any hope still clinging to the brickwork. My own crumb had long-since dissolved by this point.

I felt a vague swirling in my guts, as a familiar kind of despair began to stretch, curl up and settle there.

From what I could see, there were only two entrances to the building. One was a small, electronically-locked door for people who had the right swipe card to open it, which I assumed was the staff entrance. The other was something out of a horror movie. I could feel the despair hissing and spitting inside me at the sight of it.

It was a heavy padlocked door, thick enough to make a rampant dragon think twice about entering. Were they expecting dragons to storm the building? Even the people with appointments didn't want to go in, so why any self-respecting dragon...

I wondered, not for the first time, whether the day was coming when they would run out of reasons to let me out.

Whatever the truth of this door, there was clearly no way of getting past it until someone turned up with a padlock key.

So I waited, and I waited, and I strolled up and down the road. Various other people walked past on their way to work, giving me the once-over. Suspicious character, loitering within dragon territory, or something.

"It's not like they're taking people away in cattle trucks," somebody had told me the other day.

But as I looked into the eyes of people with somewhere more valid to go, I could see the wheels of cattle trucks starting to turn in some of them. Maybe it wasn't deliberate. Maybe it wasn't obviously malicious. But there were value judgements being processed in those eyes.

Once they'd reached their logical conclusion, there would be nothing on streets like this to hold them back. Not even dragons. The cattle trucks would be a mere formality.

I looked at my phone, which doubled as my watch. Nine o'clock - the official time of my appointment - had come and gone, with no move on the padlock. I wondered if I could still be penalised for lateness if it came down to my not having brought along some sturdy boltcutters.

There was somebody else waiting with me now, wearing the grim expression of someone who had been here too many times before.

"Maybe they don't need us now," he joked, without much actual hope - or even humour.

"A heads-up would've been nice," I joked back. Then I remembered the problem they had with phones.

At about ten past nine, the padlock was unclicked to let the scumbags in. I knew it wasn't particularly productive, giving myself that label, but all the better ones had been peeled away by the noisy fumes of city traffic by this point.

At the reception desk, I was told to go to the waiting area, where I waited. Then, when my name was called, I went over, sat down and was given a short but pointed lecture about how this was a mandatory meeting. Well, of course it was.

But given that I was already there, threatening me with a penalty for non-attendance felt like overkill. I heard the last piece of hope scream a little in the dark empty place where my soul used to be.

The rest of the morning passed like a blur, listening to things I already knew, things I didn't want to know and things I had no more stomach for knowing. They weren't words so much as mechanisms - the cogs and gears of cold mandatory functions, spilling out to slay dragons that were never there in the first place.

Mechanisms. Gears within gears. The thought stuck with me long after I had left the building... long after the drive home.

When you're treated like this, not so much by individuals as by a machine, a culture, a place where the individual becomes somehow irrelevant... well, just how human do they expect you to feel?

That evening, I was watching one of those look-how-bad-the-future-could-be movies. You know the sort. A ragged rebellion hides in shadowy corners against overwhelming odds. The powers that be pipe regular "mandatory" broadcasts into a world ruled by television screens. It's a world just different enough from our own, yet just recognisable enough...

The heroes of the film started to rally, but I found it difficult to join them. As the climactic battle began, I felt the missiles piercing the ghosts of all those things that used to look like hope. The sight of flying gunships and explosions shook loose all the things I had been holding inside, and I could feel the tears welling up.

My small life began to implode beneath the steady assault of letterboxes, phone calls and padlocked doors.

The fact is, you don't need flying gunships to break people's spirit. All you really need is a few well-placed discourtesies, all of which can be explained and justified; all of which seem entirely reasonable to people not standing where the guy with a mask of resignation seared on his face and an ache in his heart is standing.

I knew this. I knew the truth of it, and I saw no way out.

I knew what rebels and dragons really looked like - the real ones in the real world; the ones whose hearts shivered and spat on chilly streets, looking at the wrong side of padlocks and snotty letters and small procedures. I knew what was struggling to blossom in all of them, because I felt it live and I felt it die, every damn day, in a version of myself nobody wanted to hear.

I knew what it felt like when there were no words left to catch it with, no sentences that didn't seem to sting. One step out of line and suddenly you're cattle-truck fodder in every way that matters.

Whether or not I believed in dragons, I knew what their fire felt like. I saw it in a hundred different places every day, trying to say something that would never get an appointment...

and I knew...

I knew...

that it was still the only thing that would ever look like hope in a world that increasingly seemed to see it as irrelevant.

Tiny though my steps have been…

I want the world…

like when you point out all those lights,
way off in distance
and dirt,
their little colours filtered for a better slice of sky.

I want the world…

standing in a pool of streetlight,
halfway down
to something warm
and halfway through the chills we feel…

throwing little pebbles in the tide,
watching the waves
as they crunch over shells…

walking by the side of a river,
holding
what's left of our dandelion hands…

and then drifting…

and then free.

I want the world…

the way I sometimes think of it
when turning a corner means
turning a page
and painting the stories all over...

all new.

I want the steps...

the staircase I once used to carve in the sky,
when
upstairs was made out of spirals
and
bridges were made out of something unreal...

something that carried us far inbetween...

lit by the prettiest noises,
lit by the softest ethereal fire.

I want the steps...

whittled from a tiny thing
I almost used to be,
climbing a tree in the deepest of woods,
dancing with ferns
as they tickled my legs
and
finding a path up a mountain of rain,

just to see what made it cry.

I want the world...

hiding in a creaky door,
somewhere behind the intricate eyes
of someone with whom I've not spoken before.

I want the world,
not stopping like a cancelled show...

like music and rhetoric,
failing to dance.

I want the world...

the terrible coldness of old broken skies,
holding their breath.

I want what holds me,
here in the spark -
a spark whose wanton colours dance

beyond all borders...

beyond all hope.

I want a cold and kindly thing,
hiding
in puddles
and curtains of rain,
pulling apart all those star-spiral skies...

pulling apart all the harshness of walls.

I want the world,
massive though all of its terrors might be,

and all of those beautiful street-corner stars
that light up the sky when it rains into me.

The fine-tuning of unicorns

"I hate being like this," she used to say, as each new indignity stole a little more of her freedom. "I have never been so scared."

What people saw when they looked at her was absolutely not the person she had always felt herself to be.

What they saw - or, at least, what she felt they saw - was an old woman... an obstacle in a shopping queue... a victim in an armchair... something less than what might have been.

It was all too much for a woman who had always resisted the stupidity of defining people by numbers - a woman whose spirit reached so much further.

In my eyes, she was still something truly miraculous. In fact, she was probably more that person to me than she had ever been -

which I guess is the curse of a society that somehow expects people to live the wrong way round.

In a world filtered to ponies, she was what I used to call my unicorn person.

You know what I mean, right?

It's when you see something that rises bigger and bolder than anything you've ever known before. Maybe it's a cloud whose entire journey through the world's dying skies, whose entire cargo of ocean treasures suddenly explodes in your eyes. Or maybe, for the purposes of the story, it's a horse with a magic twirly horn, galloping where the traffic ought to be.

Doesn't matter what it is. It could be any one of a gazillion tiny experiences that touch you deep down in the secret places of your spirit and leave you a little closer to forever -

and you know there is only one person you can truly share it with.

So let's pretend it really is that galloping unicorn you saw.

Go to most people saying: "Seriously, I just saw this stunning unicorn!"

and they will say: "It sounds like a very nice pony."

"No, really - this was a unicorn! Had a big twisty horn and everything... glowing like a big twisty glowing thing!"

"Yes, ponies can look strangely surreal when they gallop past you where the traffic ought to be, can't they?"

You can speak unicorns 'til you're blue in the face, but they will filter it to ponies every time.

Not my sacred unicorn lady. Not her. She always heard my unicorns.

A unicorn voice will always save you from the limitations of ponies. It's the kind of voice that holds your soul together when everything else seems to want to steal it.

It's the kind of voice that tells you how needed you are, when every part of you that matters feels like it's been endlessly dissolving in its own invisibility.

It's the kind of voice that will still look deep into your eyes when you struggle to look back from this withered, lost thing you seem to be turning into.

It's the kind of voice that will tell you, over and over again, that you have no idea how loved you are, almost as though it is sharing some cosmic secret that was only ever meant to fall on your ears.

It's the kind of voice that looks deep into the wreckage of your heart, sees through the scars and the pain and the anger and tells you, without a trace of irony, that you are one of the gentlest people on the planet.

It's the kind of voice that sees what you can't see in yourself, that says you are her rock when all you can feel is a heart full of jagged stony splinters.

It's a voice that nobody but you has ever really believed in; a silence that nobody but you has ever heard speak.

At least, that's what it was for me.

It's the one thing I've ever known that really knew how to nurture me, and it will never stop living behind these eyes, no matter how many ways the world finds to burn the skies out of them.

Maybe sometimes it really does look like a gentle stampede of magic horses, with breath like soft mist curling around the mountains, and rough coats saddled with thick fluffy moss.

Or maybe it simply looks like us... unfiltered.

Rain gates

Water things,
leaping from the river skin
like frothy ripple dolphins...

Drifting mist monsters,
swallowing the mountain top...
or simply
teasing it with tentacles...

The smell of smoke,
as a bunch of travellers
set a beacon fire
to mark their presence on the shore...

and me,
thinking only of a face,
a smile
that belongs in all these worlds and more -

simply for looking into mine
and
dropping,
stone-like,
through the rain gates of my eyes.

Feather edge

Today, a part of me exploded.

Rivers of fire ran down my cheek, setting off a volcano in one of my teeth - a tooth I think I have been clenching tighter and tighter into a spiral staircase of half-slept nights. Continents shifted in sweat and nausea.

Tonight, I came crashing through the basement floor, finding it rotten like a bruised and battered molar... and I knew it would be way too long before I could claw myself out through the rubble of a house I have never really lived in.

I have met a couple of truly beautiful people this week,

sharing their company in chats just bold enough to fill the wild landscape between our lives...

flooding an ocean floor spiked and speckled with crystal minarets and sea-urchin cairns.

I met a couple of truly beautiful people, and found that such collisions still matter fiercely in the face of everything.

So now, I find myself wondering if I will ever hear from them again.

As ever, it's not my call.

If it's meant to be... so the story goes.

But I'm not in that place of acceptance right now.

I'm in the basement, covered in soft wood like chippings on a forest floor.

Though a part of me has always been aware of it, I have come to learn in the past few years just how deeply I prize my need for space.

Somebody very close to me said once that I had more need to be true myself than anyone she had ever known...

as though I was wandering further and further into some deeply unknowable place with every new turn.

They never settle easily on the page, these twists and turns of mine. Their sentences become tangled and matted between the lines.

They lie instead between my fingers like injured birds, recovering their wingbeats as I hold them. They feed off my affections, healing in fits and sparks like small birds woven out of lightning -

yet the more ecstatically I cuddle their feathers, the more desperate they are to fly away...

taking wisps and slivers of my spirit with them.

That old urge to hold and connect is still so strong in me.

I realised after each of this week's unexpected encounters just how much I hate saying goodbye...

especially once the spell of connection has been conjured...

like a fissure of lightning breaking loose from the cosmos and hurtling down from the misty peaks, a flock of electric rain and injured birds.

Part of me wants to run back to the land of giant mountains and huge empty spaces. Part of me wants to hide there, because it knows that only mountain rain is fierce enough to hold its tears.

I do hate saying goodbye. I somehow loathe the goodbyes as deeply as I seem to embrace them.

But part of me wonders whether I am someone people simply need to let go of...

kinda like the heroine of a book I read recently.

It was recommended by a friend who, I suspect, might have sniffed out the smoky scent of spent lighting from our conversations.

I found the book shockingly easy to say goodbye to when I'd finished reading it.

But those conversations...

those cafe tables and bus rides and possibilities...

It feels wrong to be saying goodbye to all those things,

to the children we still are...

still will be...

when all the buses have left and all the promises have fallen off the destinations board.

Tonight, I am tense and clenched and reckless, in need of a lightning that refuses to strike...

like a wild thing caught endlessly on the feather edge of home.

Frond stories

I came back from a trip.

I came back with stories.

I came back full.

I came back empty.

I came back with stories I am wary of sharing.

There are so many places I am wary of sharing these stories.

They are not the kind of stories people like to share.

They are not the kind of stories that start or end in the right places.

They are wild and jagged and messed-up and really quite shabby and hard to hear in places...

and they have bits in them where I needed to just crawl away and hide because of things I am still dealing with.

Because going on a trip sometimes means you have to walk through some pretty nasty, icky stuff along the way. It sometimes means you'll have to let it rip open the very part of your soul you are most desperate to protect -

all tender and weepy and raw in the face of all the scary things that are camping there, because sometimes the price of healing means feeling it until the very thing that leaves you screaming has become your lifeline.

But in the middle of all this, I find the most unexpected moments, like dewdrop bombshells dripping from vast primeval ferns.

The air is thick with such ferns here - towering fronds that curl and growl in my presence - because this place is all about presence. This place is all about space... and feel... and the things that hurt so much they eventually have to become your best friend, your lover and your heartbeat, just so the world can become whole again.

There are mountains and ferns in the vast spaces here, weaving new faces out of hot wet paint -

and I wear them all.

They trigger the beacon fires in my imagination.

I know I can't share these moments with some people, because their response will kill the magic without even breaking a sweat...

without even knowing.

I know I can't share these moments because I know just how fragile they truly are...

and I now know just how fragile and camera shy my own magic is, even when magnificent images are collapsing all over each other to feed it.

I know now how easily it breaks...

especially in the face of what people say when they don't really understand what they are dealing with.

I wrote some huge things while I was out there, in the land of giant ferns and blobby mountain monsters...

and I really wish I could make them real.

I really wish I could write the story I am trying to write now... here... in this nondescript frond of a sentence whose plaintive silence means everything to me.

But hey... what kind of a world would it be if every wandering soul with a backpack found the same mountains?

Sometimes I hate coming back and sharing my stories with other people, because they kill the most precious ones so easily.

Sometimes, finding a bottomless cleft in a mountainside, where the silence will swallow me whole without scrubbing the colours off my stories...

or a place in a forest where enchanted trees can flex their roots like claws, and the tentacles of soft woody monsters can feast on woodchip...

Sometimes, finding something that makes me feel real again...

Sometimes, finishing the day in a place like that can rekindle the sunset...

without threatening to take the sky off me...

Well, sometimes that's the greatest thing a heart like mine can hope for.

I know, now that I am back, here in the place they laughingly call everyday life...

I know the world will try to take it off me again, because that's what the world does.

Still, I live for those moments...

and those rare people...

those wafer-thin crystals of friendship...

those impossible flare beacons burning under the ice...

those devastating angels...

with whom I can share them unafraid.

A tiny rush of real

I was the one,
hiding behind the rocks where the rest of the beach couldn't see
me.

I was the one,
wearing all the wrong colours
and sewn together out of all the wrong textures.

I was the one,
hiding in a page
when nothing else seemed to fit.

I was the one,
driving down a road that didn't go anywhere
so I could sit in the car and hide again.

I chased things that didn't matter,
caught things in my fist that had no value,
and clambered enthusiastically over things that shouldn't have
been there in the first place.

I was the one,
a seemingly still point in a world of waterfalls,
standing in the rush of something...

something I could often barely see...

something that refused to set me free -

even when letting go seemed like my only hope.

I as the one
standing in the rush of something that would carry me
when nothing else could,
lifting me over the waterline
and under the clouds
as we charted our own private galaxy.

We decoded the vapour trails of passing jets,
filtering out
all those places I had never been
and
calibrating the plasma signatures of starships for unbelievable
adventures.

We bathed in the lights from far-off oceans,
eerie as the moonlight that fed them,
and cooked new stars
in the sunsets.

We frisked the beach for stories,
nurtured them with fresh rain from my imagination
and seeded them in the raw parts of my soul.

I used to be the one,
sewn out of all the wrong textures
and all the wrong colours.

But now you're here,
standing in my place,

wearing my stories round your shoulders
and
washing your hair in plankton light and surf,

so I can weave it into plaits
and rebuild my heart
in your tapestries.

Now you're here, running in my shoes...

trying to dodge all those consequences...
all the tumbles
and the lectures...

all those comeuppances that the world throws at us

for wanting to keep all the wrong colours real.

The presence I stand in

Once there was simply a wall, built out of fine rounded stones who knew their duty in the face of unrest, and knew that the only way to maintain some semblance of peace was to keep the different parts of the forest separate.

Their masters had taught them well -

and for the masters of stones and the builders of walls, compartmentalisation is everything.

Dragons, however, are all about contact. The spirit of a dragon is a frighteningly intimate thing. Its jaws, contrary to folklore, are often soft... even sensual and arousing as they clasp themselves around their victim.

But they are insatiable, too.

The dragon did not stop until it had consumed the entire length of the wall with its green, spongy presence...

dissolving everything that the wall had once stood for in a new creed of rampant streams, soft ferns and eerily twisted trees.

As the moss grew rich and heavy around the stones, its enchanted wetness soaked deep into the wall's rocky heart.

Eventually, the stones became scales... and the scales began to breathe, as is the way with dragons.

Soft and knobbly and snakelike as it was, the dragon lay in wait for any lost souls who might stray onto the path.

One day, it found me.

I was a cracked thing, leaking tears and yearnings from my core; a vulnerable thing with tired, muddy feet, looking for a place to stand.

The dragon could sense my desperation, sighing with delight as my fingertips found their way to its mossy skin. Ecstasy tingled between us, like the tingle of a pain that will never heal, waiting for you to realise that the thing you're so scared of might perhaps be the closest thing to home you will ever have.

I yielded. The dragon's coils offered me the embrace I had been waiting for, and I dissolved there.

"This is where you belong," it whispered, as I slid like a dark wet phantom through lichen-decorated tree branches and thickly-carpeted bark.

"This, finally, is somewhere you can stand."

I knew from its voice that here was a creature who understood what a struggle it is, to find yourself woven out of strange textures.

Then one day, I found a new face of sorts - a mask, sculpted from one of the fungal brackets on a rotting stump - and I stepped out of my hiding place behind the trees.

I wore a cloak of dark mist and dewdrop,

and I fed on smoke rings and wispy fluttering rainbow things and a million tiny pieces of woodland architecture whose true purpose lives only in the imagination.

I breathed an atmosphere so delicate, I thought the sobs might choke me at any moment -

but it's impossible to walk the forest spaces without crying.

Teardrops here are far more than sadness, just as the misty cowl and cloak I wear is more than just a fine weave of smoke...

just as the gills beneath my mottled brown snout are more than simply spore factories...

the air I hang in, more than mere air...

the floating, more than mere stillness.

I whisper the seeds of unspeakable things into the woodchip pages of the air...

and they dance in the presence of dragons that used to be walls, and trees that used to be dragons.

There are all manner of strange and eerie creatures in these woods, carved into the vague likeness of trees...

creatures as tall as a cathedral tower or as tiny as a whisper...

creatures whose seething tentacles can reach into the tiniest cracks and spill magic there…

creatures with fissures like those on a withered hand, reaching out for a long-overdue touch...

or creatures that stand like an ancient stag, or scream like a waterfall.

Sometimes they smile, lit up by the presence of dragons and opening full-throttle for all the Universe to see.

Sometimes they laugh, like the moment where two rivers come together and applaud their own joy...

even though nothing and nobody will ever notice the lake they have made.

There are creatures in these woods that see into all the despairing corners of the world...

creatures that hold what can't be endured...

creatures that stop where nothing else does, nursing the tingle of a pain that refuses to go away...

creatures whose very presence makes a home for those trapped in scary places.

Yes, it's all about presence.

They stand in such a human place, these creatures, and they make it rich the way only a human ever could.

They dance in it the way only a human ever could.

And when people sneer, as only humans can, at what shabby, hollow, feckless, stupid, selfish, self-destructive things humans are...

they pick up the slivers of all those lost lives that have visited the forest, and they dance over the footpaths where humans have walked.

Milton Keynes UK
Ingram Content Group UK Ltd.
UKHW020608061223
433820UK00013B/431